For Rose

Oxford University Press, Great Clarendon Street, Oxford OX2 6DP

Oxford is a trade mark of Oxford University Press

Text copyright © Stephen Tucker 1997
Illustrations copyright © Nick Sharratt 1997
First published 1997

Stephen Tucker and Nick Sharratt have asserted their moral right
to be identified as the authors of this work

A CIP catalogue record for this book is available from the British Library

ISBN 0 19 279013 7 (hardback)
ISBN 0 19 272332 4 (paperback)

Printed in Hong Kong

My Games

by Nick Sharratt & Stephen Tucker

Oxford University Press

Grab some sand in your hand,
Fill your cup, tip it up.

Empty boxes
are good fun,
They're places
you can hide,
But this one
isn't big enough
To get all
of me inside.

I know this bag,
It's my mum's.
There's lots inside,
Out it comes!

Each time I go to get the ball
It always rolls off down the hall,
I run to pick it up, that's when
It rolls away from me again!

I like flowers,
especially these.
I'll pick some
before Mummy sees.

I share the chair with Teddy Bear,
I hug him tight, it feels just right.